EZE-EGO

A PLAY

DR. (MRS) NGOZI ANCHOR-LEE OKORO

DEDICATION

To all those who knows the truth, cherish it and sell it not.

And to all my secondary school mates: Obinze Girls' sisters forever 84/85 sets and our teachers especially Sir Nwanebu, Sir Jerome, Mrs. Viola Ukaegbu, Sir Nwosu, Dr. (Mrs) Nwosu, Charity and Mrs. Virginia Njoku Our Pal among others for all the disciplinary measures.

Also my NCE course mates (1993), especially our indomitable course leader Mr. Sunday Uratuchukwu Nwosu for providing the raw material for this work.

ACKNOWLEDGMENTS

I am grateful to the almighty God for everything. My gratitude goes to my family, my siblings Iheoma, Okwudiri and Mr. Okechukwu Ugorji and their families, my friends and well wishers.

I am specially indebted to all my Pastors for their encouragement especially Professor Ephraim Okafor, Chris Iwueke, Pastor Kyrian, Rev Dr. Ebenezer Owhor. In a special way I thank Hon. Kelvin Ukwuoma, Sir. G.C. Onyekuru, Dede Astin Mbakwe, Dr Egwurugwu (Double Doc), Mr. Amara Akwari (Ochi na Nwata) May God his work in your hands.

I will not fail to mention Bro. Kelechi Ekwueme Anah, Ochinawata, Dr. Smart Mbarachi for painstakingly proof-reading the work and accepting the responsibility of writing the foreward. Barrister Vin Onyeka and Barrister Eleke, my legal Advisers, my bosom friend and mother General, Lady, Dr. (Mrs) MaryJoan Nwaegbue, it's been nice meeting you.

I thank the management, Staff and Students of Alvan Ikoku Fedral College of Education, Owerri. Sir, A.B.C. Duruako for teaching us drama and Theatre in Education. My Dean, Dr. R.A.M. Ezeala, the digital HOD, Dr. Kelechi Nwosu and all my colleagues early childhood and in the Department of Primary Education for Challenging my wits to come up with literary piece.

Finally my Publisher, Mr. Toniben for accepting to publishing this work within a very short notice. May the Lord reward your benevolence.

PLAYWRIGHT'S NOTE

Eze – Ego is a community theatre that borders on the Ezeship tussle by a young money launderer. Chief Okorobia, the Ochirizuo 1 of Akawa Community flagrantly violates the order of kingship as enshrined in the constitution of the land because of his socio-economic position in the society. This is totally an aberration of the cultural norms and constituted authority of Akawa community. Chief Okorobia and his men are skillfully used to mirror the society and point out that "No matter how people may try, evil can never prevail over the truth and justice". Consequently what happened to Chief Okorobia and his praise singers leaves nothing to be desired.

Please, find out as you read and comment your reserve.

Mrs Ngozi Anchor-Lee Okoro Ph.D

Preamble: The Igbo people are said to be egalitarian by nature. This is to say that they believe in one man one vote. From time immemorial, the Igbo man knew nothing about one man knowing it all or lording it over others. This is why one Igbo saying has it that: "Otu onye adighi abu nnam oha". The Igbos believed and thrived in the period of; "Igbo enwe eze". Any attempt aimed at imposing a lord and master on the Igbos in those days, met with stiff and even bloody opposition. This is why the indirect rule system of the British failed in Igboland.

However, today, 'Ezeship' has been imbibed by our people. With this trend came its concomitant problems- unhealthy rivalry or succession disputes, injustice, influence of money, e.tc. King makers collect money and back the wrong horse. To them, any person who pays the piper should dictate the tune no matter whose ox is gored. Brother fights brother because of money and pervert the course of Justice. Ezeship is no longer meant for the landowners (indigenes) to choose. Today, in most parts of Igbo land – both in Olu and Igbo – the thing in vague is that Ezeship is for the highest bidder; be he a Jew or a Gentile.

In this play, our attention is focused on Akawa community here in Igbo heart land. In spite of the people's constitution of 1971 which constituted the 15-man Ezeship committee making it rotatory for the three villages that make up Akawa community, an 'Udu ego' (Money bag) from the Umuodu village which produced the last eze is hell bent on becoming the next eze of Akawa community. The people of Akawa Autonomous Community know the truth but of course, where money speaks people are bound to obey. Abi ….. who no like money? …

Evening: fowls are beginning to go to rest. A man appears from a nearby bush. His dressing shows a typical traditional ruling class. His gait and an entire carpel of grey hairs show old age.

From the way he looks from side to side, the story he bears is apparently too dangerous for his health.

Narrator: (with his eyes turned skywards and presently shaking his head) Goat has eaten palm fronds off my head. Children of today no longer dance 'ipirigada' music but 'usurugada' though the latter is a spirit dance. Fowls now urinate. While human beings live under bread fruit tree laden with ripe fruits. 'What can you do? is the question of today. Ugbu m kwa: What Money can do nowadays. My name is Ichie Akataka but my people call me Ichie. I am the eldest son of the last warrant Chief of this Akawa town. When in 1971, the 15-man Ezeship committee was instituted in Akawa town, I was among the five Umuodu sons chosen. The Akawa Constitution which ushered Ezikeochie I of Akawa (the first Eze) into power

stated among other things that Ezeship here will be rotatory among the three villages of Akawa. Another village should now nominate a candidate for crowning. Now, over seven years after the death of Ezikeochie I, ego, money, Kudi, Owo …

Akawa (shakes his head sorrowfully)

DRAMATIS PERSONAE

Ichie Akataka
Okorobia (Eze - ego)
Okponku
Akirika
Ichie Nnabuo
Ichie Akunna
Ichie Nnanyereugo
Ichie Eziokwu
Ichie Akuko
Ichie obele
Ichie Oku
Ichie Nnaforo
Ichie Ozogbaku
Ichie Nnabuenyi
Egodiya
Obidiya
Chairman
Youth Leader
Member
Man
Policemen (Officer 1 and 2)
Akpobis (Jango et al)
The King Maker
Informant
Assassin 1 and 2.

Act one

A modern sitting room, spacious and well decorated.

Umuodu Village: Four men are seated. Presently, the owner of the house, apparently a money bag, begins to speak.

Okorobia: Ndi ohe Nwokekaria, I greet you all. I called you people today to discuss a very serious matter that concerns the entire Akawa Autonomous Community. For over seven years now since the death of our Eze, the Ezeship stool of Akawa has remained empty. Our people wander like sheep without shepherd. I have summoned you people to indicate my desire to occupy that vacant seat ….

Akirika: (Jumping up as if pursued by a thousand devils) Tea: Okorobia. Ishi nini? What did you say? Who occupied that throne last? Where is he from? Is he not from this family in Umuodu? Have you forgotten that according to Akawa constitution, the Egbelus will produce the next Eze and …

Okorobia: That is why I called you people. Who made the law? The law is made by the superior for the inferior to obey. Umuodu has all it takes to perpetuate herself in power in the entire Akawa community. Which human being spits out salt put in his mouth? Akawa community today enjoys regular supply of electricity, water and good roads. Who made all these facilities available? I, Chief Okorobia, Nwokekaria Ekeoma.

Okponku: But this has to do with the people's culture and unity. Akawa is not ungrateful to you for what you did for them. Is it not for that reason they conferred the Chieftancy title of Ochiriozuo I on you?

Okorobia: Do not panic, my people. I have all these things worked out. I have people in government to make my dreams come true. I only ask for you people's support. Of course, it is not for nothing I ask …

(a hitherto concealed suitcase finds itself on top of the conference table. Bundles of N1000 notes exchange hands which commands instant, co-operation from the hitherto unyielding men. Even Akirika, the first to raise objection, was sent by the money bag to the chairman of Ndioha (council of Elders in Akawa) with 'Kola' to enable the latter win the ohas to his side.

As Akirika and others leave, lights Peter out.

Act one

SCENE TWO

Ichie Nnabuo's residence the next day. It should be noted that in spite of the recent development in the Akawa community, the rich, the very rich, the poor and the very poor, dwell together. The presence of poor huts surrounding the main building in the compound denote wealth – the traditional Igbo style.

Seated in the family 'Obi' are ten men whose attire and grey hairs suggest old age. These are the 'ohas' (elders) of Akawa Community. Presently, the host, Ichie Nnabuo, a man fully in the trees of old age stands up. In that shaky but articulate voice of age, he….

Ichie Nnabuo: As our fathers say: the toad does not run out in the afternoon in vain. As we all know things are real hard these days. Money is not easy to come by. We don't produce enough to feed ourselves any longer.

What with old age and many mouths to feed. Our best option is to use what we have to get what we need. Our great grand fathers existed and thrived in the period of 'Igbo – enwe eze? But today, Ezeship is in vogue. Let us thank God that we are in a position to influence this Ezeship…

Ichie Akunna: Ichie Nnabuo, tell us why we are here when most people are in their farms or mending their barns.

Ichie Nnanyereugo: Ask him that. Are we learning parables afresh?

Ichie Nnabuo: Patience my people, patience. You people know that the Ezeship throne of Akawa community has been empty for long. Though it is the turn of Ndiegbelu to produce a candidate for crowning what can that fetch us? If a blind loses an 'udara' fruit given to him, how will he pick another? Yesterday Chief Ochiriozuo I of Umuodu sent one of his Kinsmen to me with the sum of N1 million for you people only for you to see that he is crowned the next Eze of Akawa town.

Ichie Nnabuo sits down. The silence that follows is deafening. The entire 'oha' look at one another in a did-you-hear-that-way. Of course, money speaks and rules the world. Certain agreements are made without altering a word. This is one of them. N1 million for 10 wretched elders just for their co-operation.

But, as the saying goes, in every twelve there must be a Judas. So it is time to let go of silence from the meeting. Although the money is enticing, the heart is another determinant factor in its acceptance. Ichie Eziokwu's heart troubles him so much that he speaks out...

Ichie Eziokwu:: Fellow elders, it is said that the grey hair is a sign of wisdom and wisdom they say is the principal thing. Wisdom is profitable to direct, correct and instruct. I think we should not allow money to rob us of our integrity. As you all know, the village has given us their trust and we can't afford to fail them. Trust is almost impossible to earn when broken. They are looking up to us as people of justice. Let's not fail them by allowing money to tear us apart. We should think twice on this issue. The whole village is watching and will use it to judge our posterity when we are gone.

Ichie Akuko: (Clears his throat). Ichie you have spoken well though it was a long sermon. My fellow elders, I greet you all. (They respond). I think we should go home and meditate on this. It is true that it is between our integrity and shagarin but we have to think twice. Money is the juice of life. We have to think on the possibility of not losing both. That is why we are called Ndi Ichie.

Ichie Nnabuo: Fellow elders, it is said that elders do not make mistakes, at least, not in everything. It is also said that what a child sees standing up; the elder has seen seating down. I believe we all know what Chief Okorobia, the Ochiriozuo 1 of Umuodu is after. I also believe we got the message his errand boy (He touches the bag of money) is here to deliver. Let's rally our support round him. Since he started this way, it means he will do more. This is just the beginning. However, I will still give us all time to think about it before we strike a balance. Maybe in our next meeting, we would have known the way our minds lead us.

Ichie Nnabuo dismissed the meeting when he finished because none was talking again but whispers from behind.

Light fades away

Act one

SCENE THREE

The cock reminds Ichie Obele that the day has broken. He searches round his bed for his walking stick to support his aging bones. He reaches for his companion who helps him stand up. (Now outside the house) Ichie Obele is unhappy because of the untidy premises of his house, the door to the house of his wives are still locked.

Ichie Obele: Obidiya! Obidiya!

Obidi ya: Yes, Nna anyi

(She dashes out of the house with sleepy eyes)

Ichie Obele: So you people have conspired to turn my surrounding to a refuse dump? What is the matter with the two of you?

Ulumma: No, Nna anyi. We are sorry.

Ichie Obele: It is so unusual of you. (He points at Obidiya, his first wife) You people should quickly tidy this .place. I may be having visitors and will not want them to see my homestead like this.

(He washes his face and mouth with water, leaves for his Obi, to perform his morning rituals.)

Ichie Obele was able to scale through the little staircase of his Ob] with the help of his walking stick, after he discovers it was not as usual and age is really telling on him. At first, he couldn't believe his eyes. He tries again and again before the doubt clears his mind. He couldn't believe that he could no longer easily climb the staircase he just climbed yesterday. All thanks to his ancestors who keep reminding him of an imminent reunion with the happenings around him. He enters his Obi, a not-too-scanty chamber with few sofas. He sit on his seat, reaches for his bottle of liquor and kolanut which are within close range of the hand. When he gets them, he keeps them together like newly wedded couple at the church altar . He washes his face and mouth, then, begins his morning libation...

Ichie Obele: Eke, Orie, Afo, Nkwo, greatest ancestors of the entire Igbo race, this is for you. (He pours out some liquor and let go of some kolanut to appease them). Obele Ochie, Obele Ugwu, Obele Ovi, Obele Ndicha, Obele Ekezie, I have come this morning. As usual, this is for you. (He sends off some liquor again with some kolanut, then begins). Onye si anyi adila agaghi adi. Uzo sara asa. Onye si anyi etinyela isi, uzo kporo ya. Egbe bere, Ugo bere, nke si ibe ya ebela, nku kwaa ya. . .

He is about ending his morning libation when his friend Ichie Eziokwu enters.

Ichie Eziokwu: Ichie Obele! Ichie Obele!

Ichie Obele: Who must be calling by this time of the day? Has the mother fowl committed sacrilege? Wait, that sounds like the voice of my good friend Eziokwu. (He hurries to direct the caller.)

Ah! Ichie Eziokwu, I am here. Please come over to my Obi.

Ichie Eziokwu: Oh, Okay

Ichie Obele: Ehe, welcome my good friend. What brings you out by this time of the day? I know it must be serious. It is said that the frog does not run in the afternoon in vain. I have kola here if you don't mind.

Ichie Eziokwu: Thank you my friend. Sorry for the early morning visit. I have come to discuss with you about the issue of the last meeting. I am beginning to get bothered by Ichie Nnabuo's close association with Chief Okorobia these days. I am smelling a foul play. I think he is trying to deny the people of Ndi-egbelu their right. Though I am from Umuodu, I don't support injustice. He may be wealthy but justice matters a lot because we do not know who will be next tomorrow. It may even be the turn of our children tomorrow. We need to maintain good record because once it's broken, the center cannot hold again. Once we permit the corruption to permeate, it will stay and never to go away. So, we need to stop it.

Ichie Obele: Ichie, you have spoken well. We should stand against this atrocity. Even if we accept it, the 15-man Ezeship committee won't agree. But ... (He looks upwards with his right hand romancing the beards of his jaw) We can gain from both sides.

Ichie Eziokwu: How? I hope you are not trying to take sides with Ichie Nnabuo?

Ichie Obele: Ah ah, you don't trust me again? It is simple. We collect the money since he has enough to spare and support the 15-man Ezeship committee's decision. Simple! My father taught me not to reject money. So, we accept it and back the committee. Finish! There's no big deal there.

Ichie Eziokwu: There's sense in what you just said but you know, we have to be present on that day.

Ichie Obele: (He smiles) that's not a problem. Leave it to me. Already, I am working closely with the Chairman and members of the 15-man Ezeship committee.

Ichie Eziokwu: Ichie dike! (He hails). You are wisdom personified. With you, there's no need to panic.

Ichie Obele: They will know why I am called Ichie Obele since they decided to shame the 'Oha' (He laughs). Enweghi ihe n'eme.

Ichie Eziokwu::   Ichie dike! I will be taking my leave to the farm. Will be waiting for the next meeting to get my own portion of the ego oil (Oil money), Ichie_dike! Imeela.

(Curtain falls)

Act two

SCENE ONE

The day is at its peak, the trees dancing to the song of the wind while the leaves keep cheering them. Ichie Nnabuo is sighted comfortably relaxing under one of the shades, watching a cock chasing after a hen for the satisfaction of its inborn hunger. It is said that a fall awaits one in hot pursuit of a fowl and I ask, what awaits a cock after a hen? This left for you to decipher. In same hand, the air is all over the leaves, making love to them and also doing same all over Ichie Nnabuo. Some footsteps distract him.

Ichie Nnabuo: Ichie Nnabuehi, it is good to see you. Welcome, my fellow elders. Please, come with me to my Obi. (He stands and they follow him)

(The Obi of Ichie Nnabuo is like the Obi of one

who has touched money before. Eventhough it can't be compared to that of Chief Okorobia, considering his opulence. It is still manageable

Ichie Nnabuo: (bringing some kolanuts). This is kolanut Ndi Ichie.

Ichie Akuko: Thank you very much Ichie. We accept it with a grateful heart. (They bless the kola and begin to eat. While they are eating, Ichie Nnabuo asks...

Ichie Nnabuo: To what do I owe this visit?

Ichie Akuko: Ichie, all is well. Do not fret. We have come to see you concerning the last issue we discussed in our last meeting.

Ichie Nnabuo: (Smiling) Yes?

Ichie Akuko: we have come to show solidarity with Chief Okorobia after meditating on what he has achieved so far.

Ichie Oku: He demands a second chance with his grand achievements. He has done so much for the village. As people of conscience, we can't deny him this opportunity.

Ichie Nnaforo: Exactly! We can't. (He says pointing his staff to the ground to show solidarity with Ichie Akuko's statement)

Ichie Ozogbaku: Ichie Nnabuo, you are not saying anything. You have just been smiling. I hope we are making sense?

Ichie Nnabuo: You are making sense my elders. I am smiling because you have begun to see my reasons for tipping my toe for him. I have long expected your turn up. Now, I am glad you have realized yourselves. Don't mind Ichie Eziokwu and Obele. They will soon join us. This is an offer we can't afford to reject.

Ichie Nnabuehi: (Finally speaks). We can't o. I need that money to assist my child travel to Ameica…(it was deliberately used to portray his ignorance)

Ichie Nnabuo: You mean America?

Ichie Nnabuehi: Yes! America (they all laugh). My son will go there and bring back money like Chief Okorobia.

Ichie Nnabuo: He will, my Ichie. Who doesn't need money? As for Ichie Akunna and Nnanyereugo, I will take care of them.

Moreover, we know the majority carry the vote. Even if they don't give in, we will share their part and have more money.

('More money', they all repeat, rejoice and part ways)

Act two

SCENE TWO

A new day sparks with boisterous activities. People are seen walking to and fro to meet up with the day's requests. Chief Okorobia and Mazi Akirika walk into Ichie Nnabuo's compound.

Akirika: Ichie dike! (He calls)

Ichie Nnabuo: Who is that?

Akirika: Ichie dike! It's me Akirika (Ichie comes out)

Ichie Nnabuo: Oh! Akirika. Ah! You came with Chief Okorobia? You are all welcome. Come in. (He ushers them in and beckons on his wife Ego, to get him some kolanut).

Egodi ya: Nna anyi, here is the kolanut.

Our visitors you're welcome.

Okorobia: Thank you Nne anyi.

(She excuses herself while the men continue their conversation).

Ichie, thank you for the kolanut. our people say that he who brings kola, brings life. Thank you for the life you bring to us. (He blesses the kola and they begin to do justice to it while keeping the conversation alive),

Akirika: Ichie dike! We have come to know how far you have gone with the awareness campaign among the 'Oha' and to know the challenges if any. You know the deal day is fast approaching and we are doing our best to get things done.

Ichie Nnabuo: Yes. Akirika. Thank God you came with Chief Okorobia. You people don't need to worry. I was the one who gave you this idea. Already, I have succeeded in bringing over six (6) out of the ten (10) members of 'Oha". Though two are adamant on not following us, and the other two indecisive, I will do my best to buy all of them over.

Okorobia: Ichie, I need them to come over. Please, what again can I do to get them on our side? Just tell me. Even if it means increasing their share, I will. Maybe others may have given them more. I am ready to give them more than they were given.

Ichie Nnabuo: Okorobia, you may choose to add more. I will still go and meet them after the meeting depending on its turn out but I am positive it will go well. Be positive about it. Nevertheless, you don't need to be afraid. In 'Oha', the majority carry the vote. You don't need to disturb yourself because the majority is already on your side.

Akirika: Ichie dike! I trust you. I know your capacity.

Okorobia: In that case, I will. (He brings out more bundles of cash and hands them over to Ichie Nnabuo. While some are meant for the increase of other Ichies own, others for Ichie Nnabuo).

Ichie Nnabuo: Ah! Again? Okorobia nna a, ina-eme nke ahuru n'anya. You are the true son of your father. Who says you won't inherit the throne? That person doesn't know the power of 'Oha'. It is settled.

The three men exchange pleasantries. Immediately they w^rere done. Akirika and Chief Okorobia head home.

(Curtain falls)

Act two

SCENE THREE

Akirika and Chief Okorobia meet Ichie Eziokwu and Ichie Obele on their way home. The two groups exchange greetings. Ichie Obele asks them how their fellow Ichie, Ichie Nnabuo is doing and they respond positively. The two Ichies quickly dismiss them in order to catch up with
time.

Akirika: Chief, it is working. Kai! Didn't you see how they were happily looking at you? I know they are heading to Ichie Nnabuo's house. I trust Ichie. He will do the rest.

Okorobia: You are a wise man Mazi Akirika. In fact, when I am crowned King, you will be my right-hand man.

(The men leave the stage)

Ichie Obele:	Ichie, your suspicions are right. That is what they do. They keep meeting Ichie Nnabuo secretly. Ha! Ichie Nnabuo, who bewitched you? He is becoming a disgrace to Ndi Ichie.
Ichie Eziokwu:	My guess has never failed me before. They may be thinking we are going to Ichie Nnabuo's house but their guess is wrong. Let's hurry before Ichie Nnanyereugo leaves the house.

The two men walked faster in order to meet Ichie Nnanyereugo before he goes to farm. On their way, they met a lot of people who kept pouring in greetings more than they could exhaust. They reached the house of Ichie Nnanyereugo and found him outside the house with Ichie Akunna.

Ichie Obele:	My dear elders.
Ichie Akunna:	Who do we have here? Ichie Obele of the great Kingdom of

Akawa.

Ichie Obele: My own elders.

Ichie Nnanyereugo: You are highly welcome friends. (He gives them a seat). Maybe we should go inside the house

Ichie Eziokwu: (Protests) No, no, no here is okay. Don't disturb yourself Ichie. Here is very good. Chukwu Okike has really scheduled our meeting to hold here. We were planning how to meet Ichie Akunna but Chukwu Okike took control. Ichie Akunna, ya gaziere gi. Without further delay, we have come in regards to the last discussion we had in our last meeting.

Ichie Akunna: O! You mean Chief Okorobia's demand? Exactly! (He exclaims

	with a nod of his head)
Ichie Nnanyereugo:	That's not even a problem. I cannot watch that abomination take place. I can't join them. It is an abomination because no just mind would accept it. Personally, I am going against the move.
Ichie Akunna:	(Clears his throat). Nnanyereugo has spoken well. I cannot support that evil, money or no money. When one eats, he permits others eat too. Umuodu has eaten. It is the turn of Ndi-egbelu. They should permit them eat too. They shouldn't be denied their turn. If we join in this atrocity, we should prepare to surrender next time.
Ichie Eziokwu:	In that case, I think we should rally round Ndi-egbelu and the 15-man committee. We have to

prepare fast because I know they have been preparing. If we don't stand for justice and against this injustice now, our ancestors will not forgive us. They will not welcome us in the land of the spirits. We have to take steps to solidify our stand. We have already been in contact with the 15-man committee and the leaders of Ndi-egbelu.

Ichie Obele: We have all spoken well. The next is action. We need to match action with our words. My fellow elders, may you live long. I am strongly in support of our views but my late father taught me not to reject any good offer especially when money is in question, I am not saying/taking sides with them. Never! May our ancestors forbid that. All I am saying is that we should not spit out the sugar forced into our mouths. They know we won't agree to their demand but since they still insist on bringing the money, then, who are we to reject it?

Ichie Nnanyereugo: You have spoken well. Your view is perfect but I think, collection is a sign of acceptance. Once we collect the gift from them, they will count it as acceptance of their move.

Ichie Obele: Who cares? Since we have made it known to them through our personality and they insist, then we have to show them that there many ways to kill a rat.

Ichie Akunna: Ride on Ichie. There's sense in your words.

Ichie Nnanyereugo: I am not saying that you are

wrong. What I am trying to say is that this is a Greek gift. We should reject it. For me, I will not accept it from their hands. (Ichie Obele takes note of the phrase for documentation and proper interpretation).

Ichie Eziokwu: Anyway, you have hit the harmer on the nail Ichie Nnanyereugo.

Ichie Akunna: The money issue should not be a problem. The most important thing is letting them know our stand. It is letting them know we are not in support of the move. I should be going soon. I will be having a visitor very soon,

Ichie Obele: It is necessary we don't allow this issue to tear us apart. We have to buckle up and face other important things. This is not too important as we take it. It is a matter of playing the game well. Since the 15-man committee members and the leaders of Ndi-egbelu are aware of their grand plan, we have nothing to worry about. We just have to make sure the manna doesn't bypass us since Okorobia has enough of it. Maybe he is the one that packed the remaining manna the children of Israelites couldn't gather before God destroyed the rest. We have to dismiss and attend to other issues.

(Curtain falls)

Act three

SCENE ONE

Outside Ichie Nnabuo's house, the elders 'Oha' meet again. The trees are seen rejoicing over the decision that will be taken. The cocks sound their trumpet-like voices. The birds of the air sing panegyric songs in praise of the few men of valour. Ichie Nnabuo stands and speaks. . .

Ichie Nnabuo: Fellow elders, I welcome you all to this very all important meeting. It is a very important meeting because on it hinges the needed change we want in our land. That is why it has brought us together again a little earlier than expected. Our people say that there is no smoke without fire. Already, we know the fire and we need to take necessary steps to quench it. Today again, I present to you the gift from Chief Okorobia as I hear your opinions on what to do. (He seats)

Ichie Akuko:

There is no need for wasting of time again. We all know his demand. If you have any different view, air it. Ichie Nnabuo has played his own part by delivering to us the message from Chief Okorobia. It is now our turn to speak. Let's not waste time. For me. I have nothing to say.

Ichie Nnanyereugo:

I greet you all Ndi Ichie ibe m. I don't know why this matter is brought before us in the first place, knowing we have a custom that guides us. This is an abomination. It has never happened before. Do you think our ancestors will be happy with us if we support this daylight evil? Let's not sell our integrity, pride and conscience for money. For me, I don't support Chief Okorobia's demand. It's unfair if we do. O gaghi ekwe omume.

Ichie Eziokwu: I don't know what has befallen us. This kind of matter should not even be heard among us, let alone being a point of discussion. It is an "aru". I don't want our ancestors to reject me in the land of the spirits when I die.

Ichie Akunna: I believe we have all heard

	ourselves and known who stands where. I think it is high time we discussed something else. If there's nothing else, let us all go home.
Ichie Oku:	My fellow Ichie, we have not asked anybody not to go home. To the best of my knowledge, none has stopped any from going home, so, if you want to go, please go and allow others relax.
Ichie Akunna:	(Stands) Ichie Oku. are you talking to me like that?
Ichie Oku:	I couldn't remember ever mentioning your name.
Ichie Obele:	(Intervenes) Ndi Ichie, we don't have to behave this way. When a child reacts like a child, we know it is the childish mentality at work but when an elder reacts like a child, how do

we explain it? There is no cause for verbal attack and counter-attack here. We have all known ourselves. My father taught me not to reject money. Since it is a gift from Okorobia, I think there is no need to reject it. Silence they say means consent. I say, silent is consent.

Ichie Nnabuo: Fellow elders, just as Ichie Obele has said, there is no need for us to insult ourselves and no need to panic. This is just a gift to thank us for being good elders of the land. Since there is no other agenda, I will quickly share the money so that we start going.

(He opens the bag of money and begins to share it while Ichies Nnanyereugo, Akunna and Eziokwu take their leave)

Ndi Ichie where are you going? I thought we all agreed.

Ichie Oku: Leave them alone. Let them go biko.

He shares the money to all present and keeps the portion of those absent. He did this because he promised Chief Okorobia that he will put extra efforts by going to their houses to convince them.

As those present receive theirs, they go home. When others left, Ichie Nnabuo noticed that Ichie Obele has not gone despite receiving his. He asked him.)

Ichie Nnabuo: Ichie Obele, is there any problem or is there anything you want us to discuss?

Ichie Obele: There's no problem Ichie. I stayed to get the portion of those absent and deliver it to them.

Ichie Nnabuo: (Surprised) Ichie Obele what are you saying? Those absent? They clearly stated their minds. They said they can't partake of it.

Ichie Obele: You know we are good friends. I know how to speak to them and when I speak, they listen. Just give me their portion and trust me, I will deliver it to them. I will visit them one by one.

Ichie Nnabuo: Are you sure they will listen to you?

Ichie Obele: I said that you should leave the rest for me. I will convince them to take the money. I know what to tell them and how to do it.

(Ichie Nnabuo reaches for the money and gives it to Ichie Obele with confidence that all is settled.)

Ichie Obele takes the money and leaves. Minutes later, he arrives Ichie Nnanyereugo's house and met him.

Ichie Obele:	Ichie Nnanyereugo! Is he around? Ichie dike! I have come
Ichie Nnanyereugo:	Ichie, I hope all is well? You didn't go with us
Ichie Obele:	All is well my friend. How will I go with you people? Why should I even go with you people when I told you that my father taught me not to reject money? Meanwhile, I brought your portion. The money is just a show of love from Okorobia. I also secured that of Ichie Eziokwu and Akunna. I will be heading to their houses after here.
Ichie Nnanyereugo:	Keep the stories for yourself, so where is the money?
Ichie Obele:	Ah! Ichie, I thought you said

you that will not accept the money. So you were even interested at first?

Ichie Nnanyereugo: Don't quote me wrong. I said that I will not accept the money from their hand but since it is coming from your hand, I will accept it.

Ichie Obele: (Taps him at the back). Ichie that is exactly what I picked from your statement then and that is why I made sure your portion is secured.

Ichie Nnanyereugo: (Smiles) Oke enyi m. You have always been a trusted friend. Daalu

Ichie Obele: (Smiles) I told you people not to be afraid. I have discussed everything with the 15-man committee and they agreed we accept the gifts but follow our heart.

Ichie Nnanyereugo: I have always known you to be a wise man. How much is it sef? (Receives the money)

Ichie Obele: Check it. It is more than two hundred thousand naira.

Ichie Nnanyereugo: You are truly a good friend. Thank you,(Ichie Obele leaves to give others theirs and curtain falls)

Act three

SCENE TWO

In the house of the chairman of the 15-man committee are seated the members of the committee, making plans on how to successfully carry out the coronation of a new King from Ndiegbelu community. They are also expecting the four Ndi Ichies who have decided not to permit the reign of injustice. The meeting is going on when they arrive.

Chairman: Ndi Ichie we welcome you all. Please take a seat.

Ichie Obele: Thank you Chairman. We appreciate.

Chairman: So far, we have succeeded in putting some things in order ahead of the coronation. We were waiting for you people, to know the outcome of the last meeting you had so that we can diplomatically follow things up.

Ichie Nnanyereugo: Yes. As you can see, we are here. Others threw their support for Okorobia but the four of us refused to do same. Concerning the money, we did as agreed. We can't permit their plans come to pass. We have to double our efforts.

Ichie Eziokwu: You know Okorobia may be smart. He may want to involve his political friends and the security men. We have to move ahead of him. We have to get the support of some relevant bodies, and then take them by surprise.

Youth Leader: Ichie. I agree. We need to do that.

Ichie Akunna: The youths are totally in support of justice and will never follow otherwise. We will ensure fair play stands. We will fully be on ground on that day.

Ichie Akunna: If possible, we need to get some broad-chest men to surround and secure the crown. No compromise. We are tactfully working with the kingmaker for the crown, ofo and other necessary things. Even if he insists' on neutrality, we know the steps to take to ensure that the new king emerges from Ndi-egbelu.

Member: Our revered Ichies, we believe you are doing your best as we do ours. We trust you.

Ichie Obele: We are all doing our best. We cannot afford to be a disgrace to our ancestors. We must toe the path of justice and fairness. We must defend the truth even with our blood if the worse come to worst. We must stamp our feet strongly on the ground and say No[1] to this' abomination. We must never allow it take place. We have to do our best so that our children don't question our existence in future. At least, our ancestors won't reject us when we die.

Chairman: Thank you ndi Ichie. The next thing is the place of coronation. They may be coming to the popular place. Shouldn't we *have* an option?

Ichie Nnanyereugo: They can't try that. Since

	they are taking sides with a_n Umuodu, it should be in Umuodu. Ndiegbelu cannot permit an Umuodu to be crowned King on their land while it is their turn. That is why it is rotational. Umuodu crowns hers in Umuodu when it is her turn, same applies to others.
Treasurer:	In that case there is no cause for alarm. But we have to still devise means. We should have solution to all, in case of any surprise.
Ichie Obele:	None at all. It is after the crowning in the respective places, can the King move to the palace. Even if they go further to desecrate the palace by

	crowning an Umuodu there, we will find the alternative and do ours there.
Chairman:	We have to find the alternative now.

(The meeting with the Ichies ends after brief deliberations, so the Ichies find their way home).

(Snooze)

Act three

SCENE THREE

The Akawa traditional palace. The newly crowned Ezikocha II, Chief Okorobia of Umuodu (crowned by the 'oha', elders of Akawa town as against the people's practice) is seen seated" in his Royal majesty with his Ugo-eze equally garbed and with radiating smiles sitting next to him.

As expected, the occasion is laced with pomp and pageantry. Colourfully dressed women sing and dance in praise of the new Eze. The scene of this occasion is like a fortified city. Battle-ready fierce looking police men plant themselves in strategic places. Equally, conspicuous is the presence of the new craze of modern Nigeria, the 'Akpobis' (Musclemen) to ensure an uninterrupted occasion, As the dancing women who punctuate their songs with such endearments as 'Eze-egom' 'Okorobia' 'Mbuba dike' continue unabated, the newly crowned Eze stands up, and in his beautiful regal steps, with his wife following suit, begins to spray wads of N1000 notes on the women. Petrol is poured into the raging inferno and music reaches a frenzied crescendo. Later, after letting out the traditional shout of joy, the women sit down and the new Eze............

Eze-Ego: My people, I thank you all for having made the right choice today.....

(A man bows in respect to the Eze)

Man: Eze, may you live long. I am just coming from Ndiegbelu. The so-called 15-man Ezeship committee are equally crowning an Eze for this Autonomous community.

Eze-Ego: (totally taken aback and Piqued, orders his henchmen....)

Jango: Yes, Jango Oga.

Eze-Ego: Go with your men to the place in question and ensure that no other occasion like ours holds anywhere in Akawa community. Repeat, none at all. Use any force at your disposal.

Jango: Right away, sir. (bows) turns to his men) scorpion; killer (Exchange of sign language. Exit)

Lights gradually Peter out.

Act four

SCENE ONE

At Ndiegbelu, the joyful sun honours the rendezvous of the coronation. According to the unwritten proverb of the Akawa autonomous community, it's a sign of truth, Tightness and goodness. The people of Ndiegbelu and other communities that make up Akawa community, including those from Umuodu who stood for truth, are seen dancing gleefully to the bard's sweet tunes. Also, at the scene are seated the 15-man Ezeship committee, the four Ichies; Ichie Eziokwu, Obele, Akunna and Nnanyereugo, the youth leaders and their full squad of subordinates. A combined team of security personnels are on ground. Both the young and old are seen clapping and rejoicing over the newly crowned King.

The people: Eze birikwa o. Long live your reign.

The King: Ya gaziere unu o.

Kingmaker: My King. I'm most delighted to

see this day. Today, light has prevailed over darkness. May those who plan evil against you not see the breaking of the day.

All: (chorus) Ise ee

(The celebration was still ongoing even after the King was crowned. After some minutes, a man was sighted running towards the venue of the occasion, breathing heavily as if being chased by a Lion. The speed at which he came almost made people scamper for the safety of their lives if not that the security personnels intercepted him.)

Informant: Igwe! Igwe!! Igwe birikwa o. Igwe there's fire on the mountain. Chief Okorobia has crowned himself King in Umuodu. In fact, his boys are on the way now. He asked them to make sure that no other coronation is taking place. Igwe, those boys are coming with guns and on their way now.

The King: (Turns to the informant) *May* it be well with you. However, (faces the crowd) we have men on ground. Whatever they want and anyhow they need it, we are capable.

Youth Leader: (Rises up) Umuokororbia kwenu!

Youths: lya!!!

Youth Leader: We must join the security personnels in defending the sanity of our land. We don't have guns but we have sticks. We have machetes. We have stones. One man two machetes, one woman two sticks, one child everlasting stones. We must teach every rebel a lesson.

(The people echo in agreement. Few minutes later, gunshots were heard.)

Police: Everybody take cover.

The policemen engage them. The youths escort the King and his cabinet members to safety. They arm themselves with all they can lay their hands on, then assist the security personnels.

Youth Leader: Okoro, summon the village gong man to alert the villages so that our people will be careful with movements until the situation is brought under control. Do that quickly.

Act four

SCENE TWO

The policemen gun down many of the gunmen and capture two alive. They brought them to the scene of the ceremony as people troop out in mass. Some of the youths identify the two Gunmen, rush them with beatings here and there. This action was born out of annoyance.

Assassin 1: (crying and shouting) Ay! Please o. Please don't kill me.

Assassin 11: Umunne m bikozienu, please, don't kill us. He sent us o. He sent us. Please spare our lives.

Youth: He sent you to kill us and you obeyed. Why shouldn't we kill you? You should have rejected the offer but you were bent on seeing your people sorrow. If I may ask, who sent you?

Assassin 11:   Ichie Nnabuo sent us. (The crowd roars in disbelief and disappointment.)

Youth: You don't want to tell us the truth, then, be ready for your execution.

Assassin 1:   He's saying the truth. Ichie Nnabuo sent us. (The crowd roars in disbelief and disappointment.)

Youth: You don't want to tell us the truth right? Get ready for your death.

Assassin 1:   He's saying the truth. Ichie Nnabuo sent us.

Youth leader: I don't get you. What exactly did he send you to do?

Assassin 1:   He sent us to kill the 15-man Ezeship council because they betrayed them by not taking sides with their camp.

Youth: Able leader, maybe this guys are trying to play on our intelligence. How will they say that the calm Ichie Nnabuo sent them to commit this atrocity. I suggest we beat them up even to death, so that they will know how serious we are on this.

Youth: I agree. Probably, they think we're joking. Incidentally, they're youths of our autonomous community.

Chairman: I believe they are saying the truth.

Assassin 11: Everything we've said here is nothing but the truth. Even if we are taken to any deity, we'll still stand by our words.

Youth leader: Ten of you should keep them

under arrest in the Obi until we're done with the ceremony. The gods will carry out verdict. Take them away. For the dead ones, they'll be thrown into the evil forest. Human live is sacrosanct in our land, and it's a sacrilege to kill anybody.

(Gunshots are heard. The people scamper for safety as the security men on ground engage the ^gunmen. At the heat of it, the Gunmen took to their heels while the security men went after them. The security men also called for back up.)

Act four

SCENE THREE

Jango and his men rush into an uncompleted building in order to take cover from the security men.

Jango: (breathing heavily). O boy, we are lucky. We need to rest for a while here. (Jango exits briefly to monitor the environment.)

Kapa: Guys you know Jango fucked up. He brought us here to die. He wants to ruin us and keep enjoying with Chief.

Stone: Exactly. Just my thoughts too. Jango wants to risk our lives. The security men are after us. I suspect his leave. Who knows, he may have abandoned us or sold us.

Ajani:	He's capable of doing that or even selling us out. We've to verify now. (Unknown to them, Jango was hiding behind the door eavesdropping.)
Nza:	We've to check on him now. Gbas gbos. every fuck up must be treated accordingly. We must not relent. No retreat, No surrender.

(All preparing to leave. Suddenly, Jango emerged, shoots them all to death. The gunshot attracts the security men on rampage who arrested and whisked him away. They take him to Umuodu where they made more arrests.)

Officer 1:	(To Jango) You said who sent you?
Jango:	(Pointing at him) Chief Okorobia. Ichie Nnabuo sent the first set of assassins.

Officer 11: (Orders his subordinates) Arrest them. (Jango points all of them out and once any is pointed, he is arrested.) We must be fast. We don't have time.

Chief Okorobia: Officer ,

Officer 1: Chief you've the right to remain silent. Any further speech will be used against you in the court of law. (They were all arrested and whisked away. Officer turns back to the audience.) They will serve as escape goat. To all of you into crime, know that the law spares no one. I pray they live to tell you their story. (He exits with them.)

(Light falls.)

EPILOGUE

Evil will never triumph over good no matter how people try to cover the truth. You have seen the end to tyranny. Those who through violence and fraudulent acts seek to deprive others of their legitimate rights and position will definitely be rewarded accordingly because God hates injustice and wickedness. So, if you discouraged by the seeming success of fraudulent individuals in your community and workplace, or you are deprived in any way, please maintain the path of truth. It will not be long; you will see the downfall of those tyrants and then you will know that elevation through wickedness usually end in humiliation. My people! Money is not EVERYTHING!!! Light fades away!

THE END.

GLOSSARY

Eze – Ego   Money – driven chief "Out onye adighi abu nnam oha". A popular believe and opinion of the Igbo people that one man cannot Lord over others.

Igbo Enwee Eze:	A people and a tribe that does not believe that one man knows it all as to rule others.
Ezeship:	Coronation or chieftaincy making.
Akawa:	Name of a town.
Umuodum:	The name of a town.
"Olu and Igbo":	Just like East and West.
"Udo ego":	Money bag or drum of money.
Abi?	Slangy expression meaning isn't it?

"Ipirigada":	A kind of dance or music for the young people.
"Usurugada":	A kind of dance or music for the spirits.
Ezikeochie:	The title name for the traditional ruler of Akawa community.
Ohas:	Elders.
Ndioha:	Council of elders.
Ochiriozuo:	A chieftaincy title.
Imeela:	Thank you.
Nna anyi:	Our father.
Nna anyi:	Our mother.
'aru:	An abomination.
'Akpobis':	Musculemen (Broad-chest-men)

'kwenu':   Akind of a greeting.

'Iya':   A kind of response to a greeting.

"Gbas gbos":   A kind of slangy expression used by a group of people.

Obi: A large central place outside the family house for receiving visitors.

Ichie: A traditional chieftaincy title.

Enwe ihe n'eme: Nothing will happen.

ABOUT THE AUTHOR

The drama text in your hand – EZE-EGO, is authored by no other person than Dr(Mrs) Ngozi Anchor-Lee Okoro. I developed acquaintance with this resilient and rugged, vivacious woman of multiple parts in the ordinary course of Christian life and ministry, and through association with my wife at Alvan Ikoku Fedral College of Education, Owerri, where she currently holds position as a Senior Lecturer in the Department of Primary Education.

With nativity in Okwu-Umuoma, Nekede, Owerri West Local Government Area, Imo State. Ngozi is married in Eluama, Owerre-Ebeiri in Orlu Local Government Area, Imo State. Her Pursuit and possession of the entire chain of academic qualification – NCE, B.Ed; M.A. and PhD IN English Language show the commitment of the intellectual in her.

Dr(Mrs) Ngozi Anchor-Lee Okoro, as an academic, holds current membership of several professional bodies and learned societies, including the English Language Teachers Association of Nigeria (ELTAN), the Organisation of Early Childhood Education (OMEP), the National Association of Childhood Motivators (NACM), and the Reading Association of Nigeria (RAN). She is well represented in professional achievements too, having published repeatedly in academic journals of both national and international circulation.

Before I conclude, I must mention that Dr(Mrs) Ngozi Anchor-Lee Okoro, functions in active Christain service as a Woman Coordinator in the Deeper Life Bible Church, Owerri Region. She is happily married to a name-sake of mine, with children to show to the glory of God.

Professor Kenneth U. Nnadi. Department of Maritime Management Technology, Federal University of Technology, Owerri.

www.ingramcontent.com/pod-product-compliance
Lightning Source LLC
Chambersburg PA
CBHW072119150726
47999CB00005B/2030